ANN ARBOR DISTRICT LIBRARY

31621014054825

S0-AYO-877

Ann Arbor District Library

WITHDRAWN

P

Zen Tails™

Bruno Dreams of Ice Cream

Written by Peter Whitfield

Illustrated by Nancy Bevington

Simply Read Books

It was a stifling day and the sun was beating down on Bruno Beagle. He sighed as he dragged his water pot from the river back to his teacher's house.

As Bruno trudged up the hill he saw Fur Ball licking a delicious looking ice cream.

"Hello Fur Ball!" Bruno called, licking his lips. "That ice cream looks delicious!"

"Well, you can't have any," Fur Ball said meanly, pulling the ice cream towards her, "there's only enough for me."

Bruno continued lumbering up the hill, dragging the water pot and dreaming of cool, delicious ice cream.

Bruno sloshed the water down as soon as he entered the house.

"Please Saint Bernard, I'm sweltering, I need an ice cream!"

Saint Bernard shook his massive shaggy head.

"No Bruno, you may not have an ice cream," said Saint Bernard, "you are always asking for things."

Bruno was annoyed. How could he not ask for an ice cream on a day like this? He really, really wanted an ice cream.

Bruno flopped down in the corner and thought about chocolate ice cream with banana topping, and his eyes glazed over.

Saint Bernard came up to him. "Are you still thinking about ice cream?" he asked. Bruno nodded sadly. "Well I think you should go outside," Saint Bernard replied. Bruno sighed, got up, and plodded back out into the hot day.

Outside he saw Fur Ball finishing her cone under the big elm tree, looking very pleased with herself, her mouth covered in sticky ice cream. To make matters worse, Bruno spotted Grizzel and Monkey walking over to the river, both enjoying their own delicious looking ice creams.

Bruno shook his head, and rubbed his eyes in disbelief. Everywhere he looked someone had an ice cream! Everyone except him!

In the distance Bruno saw his friend Pierre Potamus, holding an ice cream.

"Pierre will share his ice cream!" Bruno muttered to himself, and hurried over to his friend.

But when he got there, Pierre's hands were empty.

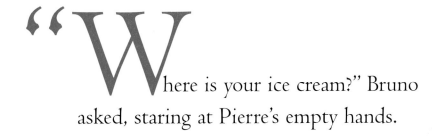

"Where is your ice cream?" Bruno asked, staring at Pierre's empty hands.

"Oh," replied Pierre, "I thought it was so hot that my little ant friends might like some."

Pierre pointed to the ground where his ice cream lay in the grass, covered in ants. Bruno couldn't believe his eyes — even ants got to have ice cream today. It just wasn't fair.

"Do you want to go for a swim?" Pierre asked Bruno. Bruno shook his head, "No, I want an ice cream."

"Come on, Bruno it will cool you down," Pierre encouraged. Bruno reluctantly agreed and off they wandered to the riverbank.

As Bruno and Pierre walked towards the river, a book came whizzing past their heads and landed with a thud behind them. "That looks like one of Gilbert's books!" Bruno cried.

Bruno and Pierre raced to the riverbank where Monkey and Grizzel were teasing Gilbert B. Beaver.

"Give me back my book, please!" Gilbert pleaded, jumping up and down as Monkey and Grizzel dangled another one of his books in the air.

"Maybe next year," said Monkey.

"This is too much fun," said Grizzel.

"Better give his books back," said Bruno.

"What are you going to do about it, little puppy?" Grizzel taunted.

"You know he's a karate champion!" Pierre said breathlessly as he finally caught up to them, "I think you should do as he says," he said nodding knowingly.

Monkey scowled at Pierre, "You don't scare us," he declared, picking up the book and tossing it back to Grizzel.

Nip Kapow Kung Fu!

Suddenly Monkey and Grizzel were flying up into the air and falling into the water. Bruno picked up the books and handed them to Gilbert.

"Thank you so much!" said Gilbert, cheerily dusting himself down.

"That's alright," replied Bruno as he patted Gilbert on the back.

Then he turned to Monkey and Grizzel who were drenched and looking very miserable in the water. "As for you two, stay away from Gilbert and his books or else I'll do more than just toss you into the water!"

As Grizzel and Monkey dragged themselves out of the water and sulked off miserably, Saint Bernard appeared by the riverbank.

"Oh Saint Bernard!" Gilbert gushed, "did you see what happened? My books would have been ruined if Bruno hadn't helped me!"

Saint Bernard who had watched everything from a hilltop, smiled and nodded wisely.

"Well done Bruno. Is there anything you would like right now?" Saint Bernard asked.

Bruno shook his head. "No no, I was just helping out a friend, I don't need anything."

"Excellent," said Saint Bernard producing three ice cream cones.

"Ice cream?!" Bruno exclaimed. "I totally forgot I wanted one!"

Saint Bernard smiled as the three youngsters enthusiastically enjoyed their treats.

"Wow, chocolate with banana topping!" Gilbert exclaimed.

"My favorite!" said Bruno as he tucked into his delicious ice cream.

Zen

This story is derived from an ancient Zen tale
about a man who went to a teacher to become enlightened.
The teacher asked him what he saw on the way and the man
described a dead donkey, rotting and smelly, lying by the side of the
road. The teacher asked the man to get the donkey out of this mind,
to think about anything but the donkey and then he would teach him
about enlightenment. The man tried, but the more he tried, the clearer
the image of the donkey became. The man found that he could not
force the image out of his head.
The teacher pointed out that this is the nature of our humanity:
whatever is taken in by the mind stays there for a long time.
To let go of all the accumulated thoughts needs discipline
and the ability to focus your attention on whatever
you are doing in the present.

Tail

It is important to focus your attention on
what you are doing and not allow yourself to be
distracted, as Bruno was, by his desire for ice cream.
Bruno was happy when he totally forgot about the ice cream.
Let go of distracting thoughts and enjoy life.

Published in 2005 by
Simply Read Books

www.simplyreadbooks.com

Text copyright © 2005 Peter Whitfield
Illustrations copyright © 2005 Nancy Bevington

All rights reserved. No part of this publication may be reproduced,
stored in a retrieval system or transmitted, in any form or by any means,
electronic, mechanic, photocopying, recording or otherwise, without the
written permission of the publisher.

First published in Australia by New Frontier Publishing

10 9 8 7 6 5 4 3 2 1

Cataloguing in Publication Data
Whitfield, Peter, 1962-.
Bruno dreams of ice cream / Peter Whitfield ; illustrated
by Nancy Bevington

(Zen Tails)
ISBN 1-894965-21-3

I. Bevington, Nancy II. Title. III Series.

PZ7. W538Br 2005   j823'.92   C2005-900577-7

Designed by Nancy Bevington
Edited by Gabiann Marin & Christina Karaviotis
Printed in Hong Kong